· THE MAGICA

NORTHLAND ·

THE WIZARD & THE FISH

THE WIZARD'S DAUGHTER

A Viking Legend

Retold and Illustrated by

CHRIS CONOVER

Little, Brown and Company

Boston • Toronto

Copyright © 1984 by Chris Conover
Based on "The Wizard's Daughter,"
collected by Svendt Grundtvig (1824–1883)
in Danish Fairy Tales (Dover).
First edition
Library of Congress Cataloging in Publication Data
Conover, Chris. / The wizard's daughter.
(The Magical northland ; 6)

Summary: A farmer's son, enslaved by an evil wizard,
is aided by the man's lovely daughter in freeing the
whole land from the wizard's spell.

[1. Folklore—Denmark] I. Title. II. Series.
PZ8.1.C75Wi 1984   398.2'1'09489 [E]   84-12613
ISBN 0-316-15314-1 (lib. bdg.)
Published simultaneously in Canada
by Little, Brown & Company (Canada) Limited
Printed in Japan
DNP

To the
Frog Princess,
who brought
good luck

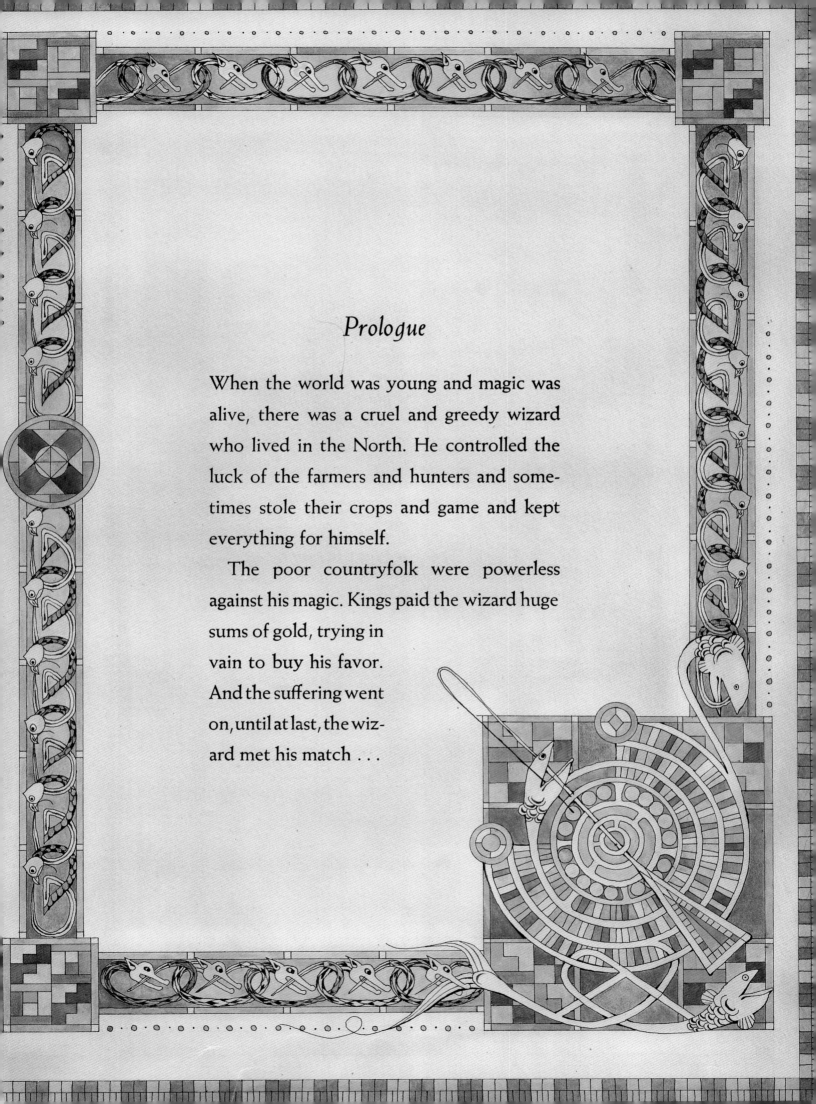

Prologue

When the world was young and magic was alive, there was a cruel and greedy wizard who lived in the North. He controlled the luck of the farmers and hunters and sometimes stole their crops and game and kept everything for himself.

The poor countryfolk were powerless against his magic. Kings paid the wizard huge sums of gold, trying in vain to buy his favor. And the suffering went on, until at last, the wizard met his match . . .

One day long ago, all the wild animals, birds, and fish vanished, and the crops shriveled back into the earth. Soon the countryfolk had barely enough food to go around, only what roots and berries they could find in the woods.

Boots, the youngest son of a poor farmer, put his belongings in a sack and set out to look for work. He hadn't traveled far when he met an old man.

"It's your lucky day," the stranger told him. "I need a sturdy lad to do some chores. If you will serve me for three years, you'll have your meals and earn a fortune in gold besides. One bushel of gold the first year, two the second, and three the third."

Boots thought, "The old fellow looks well fed. Maybe what he says is true." So Boots promised to serve, and followed his new master through a door into the side of a mountain, deep into the earth.

After a hearty meal his master said, "It's time to get to work."

He showed Boots to his stable and told him to feed all the animals. When Boots saw the vast cavern filled with animals, as far as the eye could see, he knew whom he was working for. But it was too late. He was in the wizard's power and had to obey.

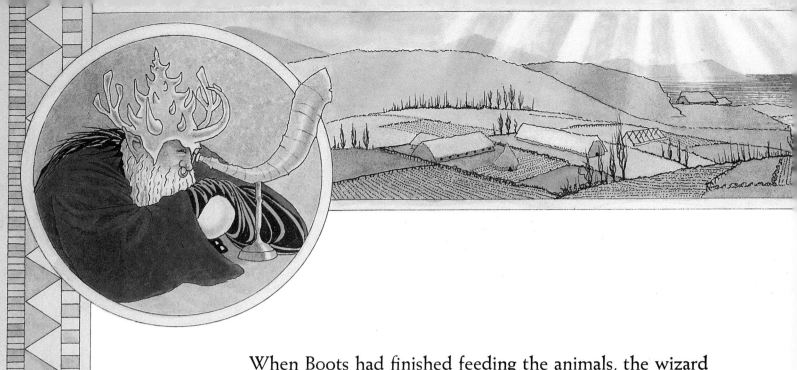

When Boots had finished feeding the animals, the wizard said, "Go keep the hunters busy until I call you again. My animals don't get such a feast every day, you know."

Then he spoke some words Boots had never heard before. Wisht! The boy became a fat hare and hopped away.

Thanks to the wizard, he was now the only animal in the land, and all the hunters were eager to catch him and take him home to their hungry families. But he nimbly kept one jump ahead and even made a game of outwitting the poor hunters. A year passed, and then the wizard called him home, repeated the spell, and turned him back into a boy.

"Here is your first bushel of gold," the wizard announced. "How did you like being a hare?"

"I liked it well enough, because I never could run so fast before," replied Boots.

The wizard gave him another big meal, and then Boots fed

the animals again. That done, the wizard told him to go back to the forest. This time, the wizard's spell turned Boots into a raven. He flew out of the cavern and back to the forest. Soon, the hunters were after him. Day after day he swooped and soared, dodging their arrows. He didn't mind at first. It was fun to fly, but he began to feel tired. At last he rested on a rocky ledge, high out of their reach. The hunters looked so desperate that he almost felt sorry for them. He looked at the huge, empty forest around him and the barren farms in the distance. How he wished he could break his master's evil spell on the country, but he knew that alone, he was no match for the wizard. After a year, the wizard called him home, turned him back into a boy, and showed him the two new bushels of gold he had earned.

"How did you like being a raven?" the wizard asked.

"I liked it very well, because I never could fly before,"

replied Boots. He was careful not to show his true feelings. And his master, for all his great power, could not read the boy's mind, and so he was none the wiser.

For the third time, Boots ate a hearty meal and fed the animals. Again the wizard uttered his spell, and this time Boots listened carefully to every word. In a minute, Boots turned into a great slippery fish, and with a flip of his tail, headed out to the open sea. He was closely followed by the hungry fishermen. To escape their hooks and nets he dove straight downward. He saw much that was new to him, but when he got to the ocean floor — what a glorious surprise! There stood a dainty palace of shimmering glass, surrounded by a lush garden, and inside the palace was a beautiful maiden.

The poor fish swam around and around, gazing at her and searching for a way into the palace. At last he found a door. As soon as he thought the words of the wizard's spell, he became a boy again, and he quickly stepped into the palace. The maiden, who had never seen a young man before, was frightened at first, but when she got a good look at him, she smiled. "Oh yes, I know you," she said. "You work for the wizard, and he is pleased with you."

"How do you know all this, living here at the bottom of the sea?" demanded Boots.

"I know what I know," she answered. "I am the wizard's daughter and I keep the secrets of his magic world. For that reason he keeps me prisoner, and only he can bring me back."

The wizard's daughter remembered little about the beauties of earthly life, so Boots described the golden sunlight and winter snow to her, and swore that she would see them one day. He told her how the countryfolk had suffered because of the wizard. They decided that they would find a way to outwit him, but meanwhile they were so happy together that the days slipped by. Then one day the wizard's daughter reminded Boots that very soon her father would call him home.

She said, "I have a plan to trick my father into bringing me up out of the sea and to end his wicked magic forever."

Boots couldn't wait to hear it. So, the wizard's daughter told him how the king, trying to spare his people further suffering, had gotten heavily in debt to the wizard.

"He will lose his head if he can't pay on the appointed day. And he can't; I know that for sure. He is more and more afraid as the day approaches, while the wizard looks forward to having him out of the way and ruling the kingdom himself. Those in the wizard's domain are already preparing for the celebration."

"How much does the king owe the wizard?" asked Boots.

"Six bushels of gold, exactly what you will have earned," she told him. "Now here is my plan. You must change yourself back into a fish and swim home when the wizard calls you. He'll restore your human form, give you your gold, and you will be free to leave. Carry your gold straight to the royal palace and offer it to your king. In exchange, ask if you, disguised as a jester, can accompany him when he makes the payment. The king will be so relieved to be free of his debt that he won't argue.

"When you and the king near the wizard's home, you will see a huge glass castle where his cavern used to be. You must run ahead and enter the castle tower, making sure that you leave the door open behind you. Do every silly trick you can think of, anything to distract the wizard from the open door.

"The day will be a long one. Before it is over, you will stand trial for your life. You must be strong and brave, and face the wizard's fury. If you can do that, I will soon be with you, and once we are together, we can easily outwit him."

It was time to go. Boots changed himself back into a fish, and the wizard's daughter let him out of the palace and watched him swim away. When Boots reached the ocean shore, the wizard was standing there with the gold. He changed Boots back into a boy, gave him his gold, and their bargain was complete. The wizard went back to his cavern, and Boots put the gold on his back and trudged off toward the spires of the capital city. There he found the royal palace, went inside, and told the guards he had an important message for the king. When they saw what a rich cargo he was carrying, they ushered him right into the royal chamber. He spread all the gold out on the floor in front of the throne and said, "All this is yours, Your Majesty, if you will grant me one favor."

The king gasped. Here was enough gold to save his life! He gladly agreed to allow Boots to accompany him in disguise. It seemed a bit strange, to be sure, but he didn't worry his head about that. His life and his kingdom would be spared, and that was what counted.

They set out the following day, with Boots prancing and cavorting in his disguise. As they neared their destination, the sky darkened. The wizard's palace glittered in the distance, decked with lights for a party. Boots ran ahead and threw

back the tall doors of the tower. He bowed low and began to caper around the room, making the wizard howl with glee at his foolishness. Suddenly, a gust of wind blew through the open door. The candles flickered; then the palace was dark. Quickly Boots grabbed a torch and scrambled up into the rafters to rekindle the huge chandelier. Just as he grasped its chain, his foot slipped, and the heavy metal ring swung across, smashing the wall of the glass tower into a million pieces.

"So, fool, you think you will destroy my treasures and live to tell the story!" the wizard bellowed. "I order you to stand trial. You must solve three questions that I will put to you. If you can't, I will have your heads, both yours and your royal master's!"

Boots, remembering what his true love had told him, climbed down and bravely faced the wizard.

"Question one": announced the wizard. "Tell me, where is my daughter?"

"At the bottom of the sea."

The wizard didn't believe that the fool knew his daughter.

"That was just a lucky guess," he snarled. He began to sway from side to side and to intone a spell, one that Boots had not heard before. Suddenly a whole troop of girls appeared, each identical to the wizard's daughter.

"Again, where is my daughter?"

Boots waited calmly. Sure enough, she touched him gently on the sleeve, and then he pulled her away from the others, calling out, "Here she is. Here is your true daughter!"

The wizard glared at Boots.

"You have done well," he admitted. "The next question won't be so easy. Question number two has two parts. First, where is my heart?"

The wizard's daughter, close by Boots's side, whispered the answer.

"It is in a fish," he repeated loudly.

"Would you know that fish?"

"Yes, bring it forward."

A hundred thousand fish burst forth, tails and fins flapping.

When the right fish swam by, the wizard's daughter pointed it out, and Boots grabbed it by the tail and cut it open.

There was no third question. The wizard, his magic undone, had crumbled into the ground, along with his ruined palace and the six bushels of gold.

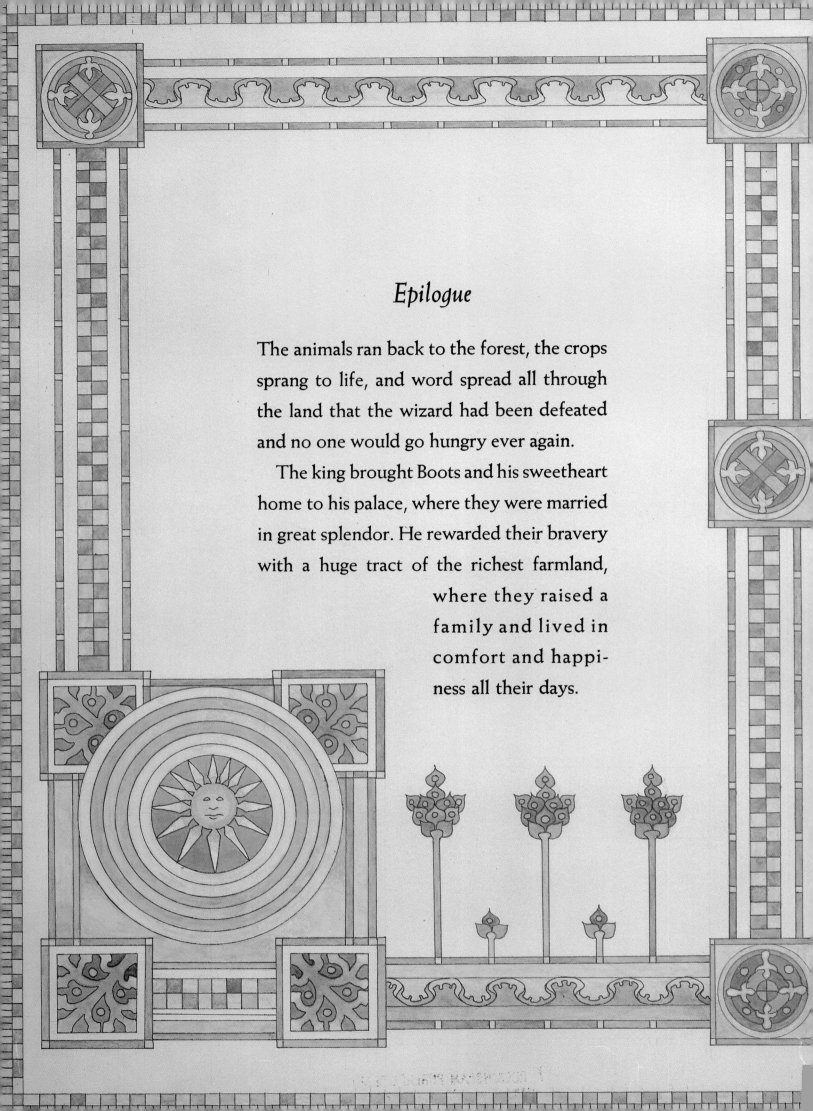

Epilogue

The animals ran back to the forest, the crops sprang to life, and word spread all through the land that the wizard had been defeated and no one would go hungry ever again.

The king brought Boots and his sweetheart home to his palace, where they were married in great splendor. He rewarded their bravery with a huge tract of the richest farmland, where they raised a family and lived in comfort and happiness all their days.

· THE MAGICA

NORTHLAND ·